PUFFIN BOOKS

What's Cooking in Spoon Stre

When Diana says, 'Tomorrow you do the cooking,' the children of Spoon Street little guess how much fun they'll have. In fact, they enjoy it so much that they decide to make a book of their recipes.

All the children's friends and neighbours provide them with lots of ideas for things to cook – such as a surprise cake for Mr Fish's birthday, an Indonesian dish to cheer up homesick Mr Nampouno and apple fritters for New Year; every special occasion is celebrated with a new recipe.
When you've read the story, you can make their recipes and learn how to cook. All the dishes are graded for difficulty and include very simple things that you can make on your own plus more complicated dishes that require some help from adults.

This is two books in one – a storybook *and* a recipe book. Twice the fun! It will be enjoyed particularly by 8- to 10-year-olds.

MIES BOUHUYS

What's Cooking in Spoon Street?

Illustrated by Tineke Schinkel

Translated by Marianne Velmans

PUFFIN BOOKS

Puffin Books, Penguin Books Ltd, Harmondsworth, Middlesex, England
Penguin Books, 625 Madison Avenue, New York, New York 10022, U.S.A.
Penguin Books Australia Ltd, Ringwood, Victoria, Australia
Penguin Books Canada Ltd, 2801 John Street, Markham, Ontario, Canada L3R 1B4
Penguin Books (N.Z.) Ltd, 182–190 Wairau Road, Auckland 10, New Zealand

First published in Holland by Uitgeversmaatschappij, Haarlem 1977 under the title *Alles kan in de Lepelstraat*
This translation first published by Puffin Books 1982

Filmset, printed and bound in Great Britain by
Hazell Watson & Viney Ltd, Aylesbury, Bucks
Set in Century Schoolbook & Univers

Contents

Things every cook should think about

First of all, take a good look at your hands. Are they clean? What about your nails?

Real chefs don't wear an apron and hat for nothing. Those lovely smells won't be quite so delicious when you find them clinging to your hair or clothes.

Always read the recipe right through before you start cooking. Put everything you will need out on the table, not only the ingredients, but the tools as well: knives, spoons, forks, whisks, bowls, pans, etc.

Always keep the kitchen door closed when you are cooking; cooking smells, which are so delicious in the kitchen, can be unpleasant in the rest of the house.

Always use a wooden chopping board for chopping and slicing. Never slice or chop directly on a kitchen surface or table top.

Always point the sharp edge of a knife or grater away from you when cutting or grating.

Never use pans that are too small; a good cook makes sure that pans are never more than three quarters full.

Always place long-handled pans on the cooker with the handles pointing away from you.

Never take your eyes off a pan in which you are heating butter or fat. Make sure that the heat under the pan is not turned up too high.

Never pour water into a pan containing hot oil, butter or fat.

When you are lighting a gas burner or oven, always wait until you see the flame burning before you turn away to do something else.

Always wear oven gloves when you take hot dishes or pans off the heat.

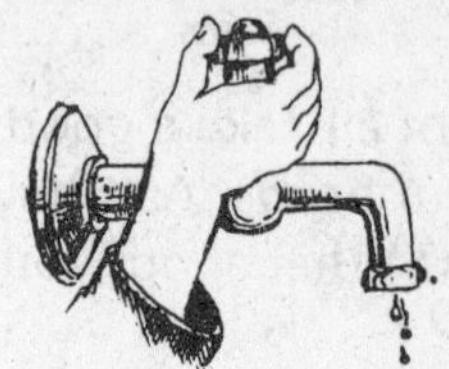

Always make sure water and gas taps are properly turned off as soon as you finish using them.

Never touch an electric machine or socket with wet hands – you could get a nasty electric shock.

Before you start doing something else, or when you think that you've completely finished, think carefully: is there anything that you have forgotten? If you always do this, nothing can go wrong.

Recipes with one star are for boys and girls who have not done much cooking before.

✱✱

Recipes with two stars are for boys and girls who have already done some cooking.

✱✱✱

Recipes with three stars are for boys and girls who are good at cooking and who would like to try their hand at something a little more complicated.

ENJOY YOUR COOKING!

Practical tips

Chopping an onion

1 Hold the onion under running cold water and peel off the papery skin.

2 Put the onion on a chopping board and cut it in half from top to bottom.

3 With the flat side down, cut each half lengthwise into thin slices. Hold the slices together with your free hand.

4 Still holding firmly, turn the half onion round and cut across the slices. This will give you small pieces of onion.

Separating an egg

1 Take two bowls which are clean and *dry* and put them close together.

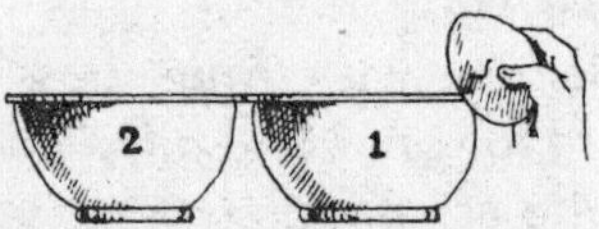

2 Crack the side of the egg on the edge of one bowl by tapping it sharply.

3 Hold the egg over the bowl and gently pull the shell apart. Very carefully pass the yolk from one half shell to the other, allowing the white to flow into the bowl. *Be very careful not to break the yolk*. The white of an egg cannot be beaten stiff if there is a trace of yolk or a drop of water in it.

4 Pour the yolk into the second bowl.

The Plan

'It's starting! It's starting!' Michael called from the bottom of the stairs. And suddenly it sounded as if all hell had broken loose in the house on the corner of Spoon Street.

His mother abandoned the cups on the draining board and rushed out of the kitchen with the dishcloth over her shoulder. Upstairs in the large front room Mrs Rosetta, the singer, stopped halfway through a set of scales, snatched up one of the brightly coloured shawls she always wore against draughts, pattered out of her door and flapped down the stairs like a large graceful bird. In the upstairs back room Mr Fish (who worked at the post office and always kept his nose glued to his stamp albums, even at home in Michael's mother's guest house) took his magnifying glass and tapped on the wall. 'Mrs Dove, Mrs Dove,' he called solemnly, 'did you hear? It's starting!' But Mr Nampouno, the student, was ahead of him. The moment he heard Michael calling he slammed shut his books and went and knocked softly at Mrs Dove's door. The old lady, who had been ready for over an hour and had been waiting amidst her house plants in the bay window, shuffled downstairs, her face beaming, leaning on Mr Nampouno's arm.

Thump . . . thump . . . thump . . . and who was that crashing down from the attic? Annabel, Michael's sister, with her friend Bianca and Bianca's brother Bas: they were still in the fancy dress finery they had found in the attic. Mr Fish nearly tripped over the train of the lace evening gown from which Bianca's small head peeped out. And then, while everybody was calling, 'Hurry, hurry, it's starting!' and they were all trying to squeeze through the living-room door, the doorbell and the telephone both started ringing at once.

Annabel opened the door for Marion, her friend from next door, and her mother snatched up the telephone receiver. 'No, no, Mr Pradon,' she shouted, 'not now. We have to go and watch the telly. Our Diana is on television! Yes! . . . Yes! Precisely. She's cooking . . . yes. *Cooking!* . . . Recipes, you know? No, no . . . now I really must . . .' She ran into the living-room, where everybody else had by now found a seat in front of the TV set. 'Here!' called Diana, and pulled her down into the seat next to her on the couch.

Diana was the only calm one present, even though she was the one all the fuss was about. Holding her head a bit on one side, she stared seriously at the screen where she was now to be seen in a bright kitchen full of pots and pans. All the grown-ups and children now hushed and watched the blonde girl on the television demonstrating how to make a cheese soufflé. To see them all sitting like that, you would have thought they were watching something very exciting: the children at the front, with open mouths, Mr Fish with his glasses on the tip of his nose, Mrs Dove nodding her grey head, Mr Nampouno serious as always, and Mrs Rosetta with red spots of excitement on her cheeks. You would have thought that the television kitchen was some enchanted cave, or that Diana's egg whisk was a magic wand and she herself a fairy who had put them all under a spell. When Diana had finished, and finally showed the viewers the golden steaming cheese soufflé, they all burst out clapping, full of admiration for the cook who was sitting shyly in their midst.

'Oh, what wouldn't I do to be able to cook like that!' sighed Mrs Rosetta.

'And me!' said Annabel's mother.

'And me!' said Mr Fish and Mr Nampouno together.

'And me!' shouted Marion and Annabel, Bianca, Bas and Michael.

Diana laughed. 'But of course you can,' she said, 'anything is possible. There's nothing to it. It's just great fun!'

'Yes. For grown-ups like you,' said Marion.

'No,' said Diana, 'for children as well.'

'The children of today can't even boil a potato,' grunted Mr Fish.

'Come, come, Mr Fish,' said Mrs Dove. 'I don't believe that.'

Mr Fish peered over the top of his glasses at the children around him.

'Now, be honest – can you?' he asked them.

They giggled. Marion looked sheepish and shrugged her shoulders. Michael exclaimed that he was only five and Bas said, 'I'm seven, but I'm a boy!'

'Honestly,' cried Annabel in her shrill little voice, 'do you think it's fair that Diana lives here with us and she teaches everybody else to cook, in the newspaper and on the telly, but she never teaches *us*?'

All the grown-ups burst out laughing and the children all shouted together that Annabel was quite right.

'Well, come on!' Diana called out suddenly over all the din, 'when shall we start?'

'Tomorrow,' said Marion.

'All right,' said Diana, 'tomorrow you do the cooking.'

'Cook pancakes for me!' Bas called out immediately.

'And apple sauce for me,' said Michael.

'Hey!' said Diana. 'If you want to eat then you'll have to cook as well. I see no reason why boys shouldn't learn to cook too.'

'Well, if I were you I'd start off by giving them a recipe for cooking a nice potato,' said Mr Fish.

'I'll write it down for you,' promised Annabel.

'And when we have lots of recipes we'll make a book of them!' cried Bianca.

'And we'll call it "What's Cooking in Spoon Street",' said Bas without hesitation.

'Children, what a tremendous idea!' cried Mrs Dove.

'A wonderful idea. *Wonderful!*' Everyone laughed, because when Mrs Rosetta cried 'wonderful', it sounded almost like a song.

Boiled Potatoes ✱

1 kg (2 lb) potatoes
1 teaspoonful salt

1 Peel the potatoes, cut out eyes and blemishes, and cut them into halves or quarters if they are large.

2 Wash them well and put them in a saucepan with the salt and just enough water to cover them.

3 Cover the saucepan, and place it on the cooker and turn the heat on full.

4 When the water starts to boil, turn down the heat and leave the potatoes to simmer for 20 minutes. Prick them with a fork to test if they are soft.

5 When they are cooked, take the pan off the heat and strain the potatoes in a colander or a sieve held over the sink.

6 Return the potatoes to the saucepan and shake them for half a minute over a very low heat to make them dry and crumbly.

Mashed Potatoes ✱✱

1 kg (2 lb) potatoes
1 teaspoonful salt
250 ml (½ pint) milk
1 egg
25 g (1 oz) butter
pinch of grated nutmeg
pinch of salt
pepper

1 Peel, wash and boil the potatoes as in the recipe on page 15.

2 When the potatoes are nearly done, heat the milk in a small saucepan. (Make sure the milk doesn't boil over.)

3 When the potatoes are soft, strain them, return them to the saucepan and mash them with a potato masher.

4 Break the egg into a bowl and beat it with a fork.

5 Add the egg, hot milk, butter, salt, pepper and nutmeg to the mashed potatoes and beat well with a wooden spoon.

6 Transfer the mixture to a dish and serve.

Fried Potatoes ✱✱

1 kg (2 lb) potatoes
75 g (3 oz) butter
4 tablespoons oil
(You may also add a small chopped onion or some chives and a few sprigs of parsley.)

1 You can use leftover boiled potatoes if you have some. Otherwise, boil the potatoes as described on page 15 but cook them for 10 minutes only. Drain them and leave them to cool.

2 Cut the cooled potatoes into slices ½ cm (¼ inch) thick.

3 Melt the butter and oil in a large frying pan and

fry the slices in a single layer over a low heat. When they are light brown, turn them over and fry the other side. If you don't have a very big frying pan, you may need to cook two batches, so save half of the butter and oil for the second batch.

4 To make the potatoes taste even nicer you can fry a finely chopped onion or some chives with them and scatter chopped parsley over them before serving.

Potatoes in a Parcel *

1 kg (2 lb) potatoes
(This recipe is especially good if you use medium-sized new potatoes.)
aluminium foil
butter
salt

1 Preheat the oven to 220°C (425°F), gas mark 7.

2 Scrub the potatoes in the sink using a small brush.

3 Dry them and then wrap one or two potatoes (depending on size) in a piece of foil.

4 Place the parcels on the middle shelf of the oven and bake them for about 45 minutes, depending on their size.

5 Before you remove the parcels from the oven, test one by pricking it with a fork to make sure the potatoes are soft all the way through.

6 Serve the potatoes in their foil jackets with butter and salt.

* *You can also cook the parcels in the glowing embers of an open fire or on a charcoal grill.*

Pancakes ❀❀

100 g (4 oz) plain flour
pinch of salt
1 egg
250 ml (½ pint) milk
oil
lemon and sugar
or lemon and syrup
or jam

1 Preheat the oven to 100°C (150°F), gas mark 1.

2 Sift the flour and salt into a mixing bowl.

3 Make a well in the centre and drop in the egg.

4 Add half the milk and beat with a wooden spoon until the batter is smooth.

5 Gradually beat in the rest of the milk.

6 Heat just enough oil to cover the bottom of a medium-sized frying pan – the pan should be quite hot. Pour any extra oil back into the jug. Using a ladle, pour a *small* amount of batter into the pan and tilt it quickly so that the bottom of the pan is covered with a thin layer of batter.

7 Cook the pancake over a medium heat for half a minute until the top looks dry. Loosen the edges of the pancake, turn it over with a spatula and cook it for a few seconds more.

8 Slide the pancake on to a large plate and keep in a warm oven while you make the rest of the pancakes. Don't forget to oil the pan each time.

9 Serve the pancakes with lemon and sugar or syrup or jam.

Mrs Dove Knows Everything

Thump . . . thump . . . thump . . . Annabel flew up the stairs two at a time.

'Annabel!' Downstairs, the living-room door opened and her mother's head peered around the corner. 'Annabel, not so loud!'

'Yes, but Mummy. I've lost our recipe notebook and Diana's coming home from the office and I quickly have to write down what we need for . . .'

'That's no reason to make so much noise. Mr Nampouno is studying and Mrs Dove is probably taking her afternoon nap.'

Mrs Dove! It all came flooding back to Annabel! She had given the notebook to Mrs Dove who had promised to cover it in plastic to protect it from grease stains, and also to attach a piece of string to it so that it could be hung up on a nail in the kitchen. Oh, how annoying that the old lady was asleep! On tiptoe, she crept up to Mrs Dove's door, pressed her ear against it and listened. Silence. She's asleep, thought Annabel, but then she heard Mrs Dove's voice, 'No, no, Puss, not on the blue cushion, you know that's not allowed!'

'Ah ha!' said Annabel, 'Mrs Dove is awake and Puss is waiting for his afternoon saucer of milk!'

She knocked softly, but just as Mrs Dove called, 'Enter!' Annabel heard the voices of Bianca and Bas downstairs, coming in through the back door. She leant over the banisters and called, 'I'm with Mrs Dove!'

'What a nice surprise,' said Mrs Dove, 'have you come for cup of tea with me, Annabel? The others too?'

'No, no, Mrs Dove, we can't today. We're cooking again and we have to go out to do the shopping first, but we need the notebook . . .'

'Look over there,' said Mrs Dove, and she pointed to the table where the book was lying ready, neatly covered and with a piece of coloured cord attached to it.

'Oh, how pretty!' exclaimed Annabel, and Bas and Bianca, who now appeared through the doorway.

Downstairs the telephone started to ring and a moment later they heard Michael climb the stairs and knock on Mr Fish's door.

'Mr Fish, a phone call for you!' he called, and then he noticed Mrs Dove's open door so he came in too.

'That's odd,' said Annabel, as Mr Fish hurried down the stairs. 'There's never been a phone call for Mr Fish before.'

'No,' said Michael, 'not for as long as I've lived.'

Mrs Dove laughed. 'Oh yes, there certainly has,' she said. 'Every year on the second of March there's a phone call for Mr Fish.'

The children gaped at her. 'How do you know that?' asked Bianca, and Bas said, 'The second of March? That's right. That's today.'

'But why?' asked Annabel. 'Why on the second of March?'

'Because tomorrow is the third of March,' said Mrs Dove.

'Old people say some pretty silly things sometimes,' Annabel thought to herself peevishly, but then Mrs Dove smiled at her and asked, 'Don't you want to know what's so special about the third of March?'

Annabel nodded, embarrassed. 'On the second of March,' said Mrs Dove, 'Mr Fish's sister rings him to wish him a happy birthday for the third of March. Well, of course it's never much of an event, because nobody else knows that it's Mr Fish's birthday. I know, and I always give him a little plant. He's always very pleased with it, but unfortunately he doesn't know much about plants and I do believe he sometimes forgets to . . .'

Annabel couldn't contain herself any longer. She quickly shut the door, because Mr Fish was shuffling back upstairs. 'Do you mean . . .' interrupted Annabel breathlessly, 'that it's Mr Fish's birthday on the third of March and nobody knows? Except for his sister, who lives far away, and you? And that all he ever receives is a plant, and never a birthday cake? And that nobody ever sings "Happy Birthday" and decorates his chair?'

The children looked at each other in astonishment. This was the strangest thing they had ever heard.

'Yes, yes . . .' said Mrs Dove. 'It never really occurred to me, to tell you the truth, but now you mention it . . . He's such a quiet man – and, well – I suppose it is a bit odd really.'

'But now *we* know about it!' exclaimed Bianca. Michael was already halfway through the door and on his way to the attic, saying that he was going to fetch the streamers.

'Streamers?' asked a voice from the hall, 'but I thought that we were going to cook?'

'Oh, Diana, Diana!' cried Annabel. 'Come on in. You must help us!' She quickly shut the door behind her. 'We can't do any cooking today, we must go and buy a cake and treats for Mr Fish . . . and . . .'

'Buy?' said Diana, 'Why don't we bake him a birthday cake ourselves? And we could cook other treats for him . . .'

'Fish,' said Mrs Dove promptly. 'It's his name, but it's also his favourite food.'

Annabel looked at Diana. 'Is that difficult?' she asked anxiously.

Diana grinned and said, 'No, not at all. And what else, Mrs Dove?'

'Limburg fruit tartlets,' the old lady said. 'Mr Fish lived in Limburg as a child and he always says, "When I think of my childhood I think of fruit tartlets." '

'How do you know all this, Mrs Dove?' asked Diana.

'Mrs Dove knows everything!' cried Annabel, who was pulling at Diana's sleeve to get her to quickly, quickly, quickly go out and buy everything for Mr Fish's birthday feast.

And the next day Mr Fish, struck dumb with surprise and delight, was sitting in his decorated chair with Annabel and Michael on either side of him and their mother, in a pretty dress, sitting opposite. The other children and Diana carried in the birthday cake and other goodies from the kitchen.

'But how . . . how did you know . . .?' Mr Fish asked.

Annabel pointed at the old lady with rosy cheeks, who was sitting watching all the fun. And again she said, 'Mrs Dove! Mrs Dove knows *everything*!'

Mackerel in a Parcel ✲✲

4 fresh mackerel, cleaned and gutted
aluminium foil
1 lemon
1 small onion or some chives
100 g (4 oz) butter
salt and pepper
few sprigs of parsley

1 Preheat the oven to 180°C (350°F), gas mark 4.

2 Wash the mackerel quickly.

3 Dry each fish with a piece of kitchen paper.

4 Wrap each fish in a piece of foil and make sure the parcels are well sealed.

5 Place the parcels in an ovenproof dish and put it on the middle shelf of the oven. Leave the fish to cook for 35 minutes.

6 In the meantime, cut the lemon in half and squeeze the juice of one half into a cup. Cut the other half into thin slices.

7 Chop the onion or the chives finely.

8 Melt the butter slowly in a small pan over a low heat.

9 Stirring constantly, add the lemon juice, a pinch of salt and the chopped chives or onion.

10 Remove the fish from the oven after 35 minutes. Carefully unwrap the foil and place the fish on a flat dish. Sprinkle a little salt and pepper on top and decorate the dish with the lemon slices and a few sprigs of parsley.

11 Serve the fish with the warm butter sauce.

* *Rice, mashed potatoes or a warmed French loaf and a green salad go very well with this dish.*

Birthday Cake ✽✽✽

150 g (6 oz) self-raising flour
1½ teaspoons baking powder
150 g (6 oz) sugar
150 g (6 oz) margarine
3 eggs
grated rind of 1 lemon

(Take the margarine out of the fridge one hour before you start.)

1 Preheat the oven to 180°C (350°F), gas mark 4.

2 Grease a 20 cm (8 inch) cake tin with a little butter. (Use a loose-bottomed tin if you have one.)

3 Sift the flour and baking powder into a mixing bowl.

4 Add the sugar, margarine, eggs and lemon rind, and beat with a wooden spoon until the mixture is soft and creamy.

5 Put the mixture into the cake tin and place it on the middle shelf of the oven.

6 Bake for 40–50 minutes. When the cake is ready it will be coming away from the sides of the tin and there will be no 'bubbling' sound from inside the cake.

7 Get an adult to help you transfer the cake to a cake rack immediately and leave to cool.

Chocolate Icing ✽✽✽

200 g (8 oz) icing sugar
200 g (8 oz) plain chocolate
2 drops vanilla essence
pinch of cinnamon
hundreds and thousands/chocolate vermicelli/Smarties/birthday candles for decoration

1 Sift the icing sugar into a bowl.

2 Break the chocolate into small pieces and melt it

in a heavy-bottomed saucepan over a *very* low heat. **Do not stir.**

3 Add 6 tablespoons boiling water to the melted chocolate and stir briskly. Remove from the stove.

4 Add the vanilla and the cinnamon to the chocolate. Mix in the icing sugar a spoonful at a time and stir constantly to make sure that it stays smooth.

5 Sprinkle a couple of tablespoons of the hundreds and thousands or chocolate vermicelli on to a sheet of greaseproof paper.

6 Using a spatula, spread the icing on the *sides* of the cake *only*.

7 Very carefully roll the cake in the hundreds and thousands so that they stick to the sides.

8 Now spread the icing on the top of the cake and decorate it with Smarties – you could spell out the birthday person's name or make a flower pattern.

9 Finally, add the candles.

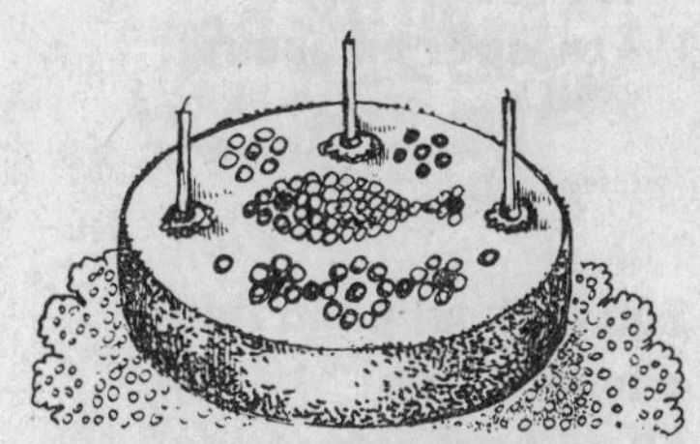

* *You can make this cake for special holidays too. For Christmas you could decorate it with chopped almonds or walnuts, and for Easter you could use tiny Easter eggs and chocolate bunnies.*

Fruit Tartlets ✵✵✵

200 g (8 oz) plain flour
pinch of salt
50 g (2 oz) margarine
50 g (2 oz) lard
75 g (3 oz) caster sugar
200 g (8 oz) fruit (thinly sliced apples or stoned plums, cherries or apricots)
2 teaspoons red jam or jelly

1 Preheat the oven to 180°C (350°F), gas mark 4.

2 Grease the tartlet tins. (This recipe makes about twenty tartlets.)

3 Sift the flour into a bowl and add the salt.

4 Cut the margarine and lard into small pieces and rub into the flour with your fingertips.

5 When the mixture resembles fine breadcrumbs, mix in the sugar and then add 4 tablespoons water a little at a time. Knead the mixture very quickly into a ball.

6 Sprinkle some flour on your work surface and rolling pin. Cut off about one quarter of the dough and roll it into a little ball. Place it on the floured surface and then roll it out evenly with the rolling pin until it is thin.

7 Cut the pastry into strips 1 cm (½ inch) wide and leave to one side.

8 Roll out the rest of the pastry and cut twenty circles from it with a pastry cutter or a cup.

9 Line each section of the tartlet tin with a pastry circle.

10 Fill each pastry case with the prepared fruit and then spread a little

jam or jelly on top of the fruit.

11 Finish off the tartlets with four of the little pastry strips criss-crossed over the top. Stick the ends of the strips to the sides of the tartlets with a drop of milk.

12 Cook the tartlets for 30 minutes.

Easter

'Splendid! Splendid!' warbled Mrs Rosetta as she entered the living-room. All the grown-ups and children of the house on the corner of Spoon Street, and the children from next door, of course, were sitting around the big table surrounded by hundreds of colourful eggs in boxes.

'I'd like to have a change from dots, stars and stripes, though,' called Annabel, who by this time was covered from head to toe in different colours of paint and resembled an Easter egg herself.

'Then try this!' said Diana, and she tore a piece from the paper protecting the table and folded it into a little pointed hat which she placed on top of a pink egg. She dipped her paint-brush into red paint and drew on the egg a large clown mouth, a red nose and two little red cheeks.

'Oooh, a clown!' exclaimed Michael. Diana went on to paint in two large black eyes and two very surprised-looking eyebrows.

'How clever you are, Diana!' said Bianca.

'Easy,' said Diana, as always. Soon everyone was busy making egg heads with coloured paper, strands of wool, and pieces of cotton wool and material. Mrs Dove proudly showed Mr Fish her Chinaman, complete with droopy moustache and a fringe made of black thread. With his tongue clenched between his teeth, Mr Nampouno was solemnly gluing some coloured feathers, which Mrs Rosetta had conjured up from somewhere, to make an Indian headdress for a red egg. Annabel and Bianca had slid under the table with a couple of eggs and scraps from Annabel's mother's remnant basket.

'I don't think very serious work is being done down there,' growled Mr Fish; Mrs Dove shook her head and added, 'There's much too much giggling; no good will come of it.'

Diana bent over and stuck her head under the table, but Bianca cried, 'No, no! Don't look – it's a surprise!'

Everybody continued to work, and then suddenly Annabel's voice came from underneath the table. 'Now! Now you may look!'

A very small head appeared over the edge of the table, a light pink egg with cheeks of darker pink and on top a neat little hair bun made of grey wool.

'Mrs Dove! That's Mrs Dove!' everybody shouted in chorus, but before they could all admire it in detail, Bianca's egg appeared: everybody recognized it immediately by the small silver spectacles made from aluminium foil slipping down over a moustache of brown bristles that Bianca had pulled out of the doormat in the hall. Even Mr Fish himself saw the resemblance at once. He looked round the laughing group with some surprise.

'But why are you laughing?' he asked. 'Isn't it a wonderful likeness?'

Without further ado all the little Chinamen, Indians and little girls with plaits were abandoned, and everybody started to make likenesses of everybody else. Marion used yellow wool for Michael's curls, Mrs Dove painted Mr Nampouno's large black eyes and looked for soft silk thread for his Indonesian hair, Mr Fish was making Diana with a red headscarf and Michael mixed different paints in a dish to find the exact shade of his mother's eyes.

Squinting slightly, Mr Nampouno studied Mrs

Rosetta's face; he painted her very precisely, her mouth wide open, as if she were singing at the opera, her big blue eyes, with arched brown eyebrows above, and her pink cheeks. Annabel's mother contributed a small piece of fine silk out of which she cut a fluttering shawl exactly like the ones in which Mrs Rosetta always draped herself.

'What a pity that we shall be eating them all

tomorrow!' sighed Mrs Dove as the heads of all the grown-ups and children were lined up in egg-cups on the table.

'Well, there's no choice really,' said Annabel's mother, 'because there won't be much time for cooking with all the excitement.'

'Hey!' cried Annabel, surfacing again from underneath the table, 'why don't you let *us* do the cooking?'

'Yes, why not? Fresh young spinach, that would go so well with all those eggs,' said Diana.

'Mmmm – delicious!' said Mrs Dove. 'Spinach! With soldiers, Diana?'

Everyone looked up. 'Soldiers?' asked Marion, 'what are they, Mrs Dove?'

'Oh,' said Mrs Dove, shaking her head, 'nowadays you've never heard of them of course, but in my home spinach never appeared on the table without soldiers.'

Diana laughed. 'I know what they are,' she said, 'and you'll have your soldiers, Mrs Dove.'

'I bet you don't like spinach,' said Mr Fish to Michael, who was looking a bit glum.

'Oh, no,' said Michael, 'I quite like it really, but I'd much prefer something really Easter-ish!'

'But we've already made the butter lamb!' cried Annabel.

'Ah, the butter lamb,' said Mr Fish, happily.

'We made it ourselves, very easily,' nodded Marion, 'from a packet of butter cut into the shape of a lamb. We made curls with a fork, used currants for eyes and two leaves from the bush in front of the house for ears, and put a red ribbon round its neck.'

'Yes,' said Michael, 'but that's just for the morning to go with the eggs and bread.'

'Wait,' said Diana, 'we'll also make a sweet, a real Easter treat. Little sweet bunny rabbits, Michael. What do you think of that?'

Michael wanted to know whether they were really sweet, and also whether they were too difficult for a five-year-old to make. Diana laughed, and said, as always, that there was nothing to it.

'It's going to be a jolly Easter,' said Mrs Dove to Mr Fish. 'Everybody's happy, you with your butter lamb, me with my soldiers and Michael with his sweet bunny rabbits.'

'It simply couldn't be better,' said Mr Fish.

Sweet Bunny Rabbits ✱

1 packet of green jelly
pear halves from a tin
blanched almonds
glacé cherries
currants or raisins
a little sweetened whipped cream

1 Make the jelly according to the directions on the packet and put it in the fridge to set.

2 Open the tin of pears and drain off the juice.

3 When the jelly has set, chop it up roughly and spread it on a large plate.

4 Place the pear halves, flat side down, on top of the chopped jelly.

5 Using the narrow end of the pear as the rabbit's head, push the almonds in to make ears. Make a little round red nose with a glacé cherry, and eyes with the currants or raisins.

6 Finally, decorate the other end of the pear with a little blob of stiffly whipped cream to make a fluffy tail.

Spinach with Ham Rolls and Soldiers ✱✱✱

1.5 kg (3 lb) spinach
4 slices white bread
50 g (2 oz) butter or margarine
1 small onion finely chopped
pinch of salt
25 g (1 oz) plain flour
200 g (8 oz) sliced ham

1 Preheat the oven to 180°C (350°F), gas mark 4.

2 Wash the spinach well in plenty of water.

3 Put the wet spinach leaves in a large saucepan. Don't add any more water.

4 Cover the pan with a lid and bring the spinach to the boil.

5 As the spinach starts to shrink, turn the leaves over with a wooden spoon.

6 Reduce the heat and continue to cook gently for five more minutes.

7 While the spinach is cooking, cut the crusts from the bread and cut each slice into four strips.

8 Heat the butter in a frying pan until it is golden brown.

9 Fry the chopped onion in the butter until soft, then remove from the pan with a spoon and put it on a plate. Using the same pan, fry the strips of bread on both sides until they are golden brown. These are your soldiers.

10 Drain the spinach in a colander. Press it down with a wooden spoon to get out as much water as possible.

11 Place the spinach on a chopping board and chop it finely. Return it to the pan, add the fried onions and salt, sprinkle on the flour and mix well. Cook for a few minutes.

12 Place a little spinach on top of each slice of ham and roll it up like a fat sausage.

13 Grease an ovenproof dish. Put the filled ham rolls in the dish.

14 Place the dish on the middle shelf of the oven and heat it for 10 minutes. Just before serving, arrange the soldiers around the ham and spinach rolls.

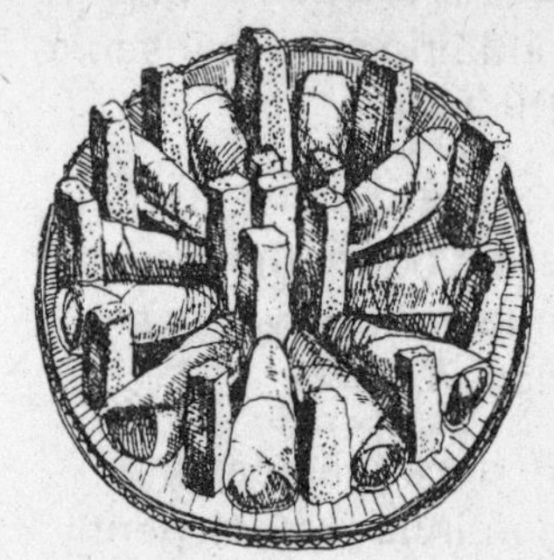

* *You can also serve the rolls on rice or mashed potato.*

The Sun in a Pan

'One, two, three, four . . .' Annabel sat on the kitchen work-top, dangling her legs.

'Whatever is it that you keep counting?' asked Diana, who was sitting down to breakfast with Annabel's mother.

'The recipes of course!' said Annabel, 'nine, ten, eleven, twelve . . . Does that make enough for a book yet, Diana?'

Diana laughed. 'No, I don't really think a cookery book containing only twelve recipes would be useful to other children. You'll have to go on cooking for almost another whole year before you have enough.'

Annabel looked crestfallen. 'But doesn't it take an awfully long time to finish a book? Your own cookery book took at least a hundred years before it finally appeared in the bookshop.'

'Oh Annabel,' said her mother, 'you're always so impatient! The book will be ready when it's ready, but if I were you I'd go and fetch my satchel this very minute, because Marion and Bianca and Bas will soon be here to pick you up on their way to school.'

Diana hastily put down her cup. 'Is it that late?' she asked. 'I have to be at my publishers' at nine o'clock and it's . . .'

'Oooh!' interrupted Annabel. 'Then you can talk to them about our book at the same time!'

'Wait a minute,' said her mother, who was standing in the middle of the kitchen with the coffee-pot. 'Half-past eight? I wonder why Mr Nampouno isn't down for breakfast yet?'

'Oh, he's probably not hungry again,' said Annabel. 'Did you see him yesterday, Mum? He hardly had any of that lovely cauliflower!'

Annabel's mother sighed. 'Well,' she said, 'sometimes I just don't know what to do about him. He studies so hard, he never goes out, not even to get some fresh air . . .'

'What's the point, with all this rain?' asked Annabel.

'Do you know, Mum, the weather has been awful for two whole weeks now?'

Her mother nodded. 'Yes, that's why I'm so worried about Mr Nampouno. He looks so pale, and he has that cough . . . People who come from hot countries need the sun more than we do. Run upstairs, Annabel, and knock on Mr Nampouno's door. Ask him whether it isn't time for him to get up.'

Annabel knocked and put her ear to Mr Nampouno's door. She could hardly make out his voice calling, 'Come in!', it was so strange and hoarse. She opened the door cautiously and was startled by the thin pale face above the bedclothes.

'You're ill,' she said.

'Yes,' said Mr Nampouno, hoarsely. 'I think I am, Annabel.'

'You ought to eat more and go out and have some sun and things,' said Annabel sternly.

Mr Nampouno laughed weakly. 'The sun, Annabel? Where do I find that?'

Annabel was unable to answer that question, so she said, 'You must stay in bed and I'll call my mother. And you *must* eat!'

Because it was Wednesday, the half-day at school, the children were not surprised to see Diana's little red car waiting for them outside school at twelve o'clock. She often picked them up from school on a Wednesday because they did their cooking in the afternoon, and they could go shopping on their way home.

'How is Mr Nampouno?' Annabel asked her.

'The doctor has been,' Diana told her. 'It isn't too bad. He's been told to eat sensibly. And he needs some sun, of course.'

'I wish we could bring him some sun,' said Annabel, who couldn't get Mr Nampouno's pale face out of her mind. The others laughed at her, but she stayed serious.

'No, really,' she said. 'The bad weather is much worse for him than it is for us. In his country the sun shines all the time. Last week I saw him looking out of the window at the grey skies and he said, "I can hardly believe that it's different elsewhere. At home everything tastes and smells of the sun: the gardens, the houses, the food – but with all this rain, I've quite forgotten what it smells like . . ." '

The others had stopped laughing, and you could see that Diana, at the wheel, was thinking. Suddenly she said, 'Annabel's right, you know. We should bring him some sun – the sun in a pan – to help him remember what home smells like!'

The children looked at each other in surprise. What did that mean? The sun in a pan?

At six o'clock that evening Annabel and Michael knocked softly on Mr Nampouno's door. They were afraid that he might be asleep, but when they peered through a chink in the door they could see him sitting up in bed looking a lot better.

'Aren't you ill any more?' asked Michael, who had crept round the house on tiptoe all afternoon.

'I'm nearly better,' said Mr Nampouno. 'I slept so well!'

'Did you dream?' asked Annabel while she busied herself laying the table next to the bed. Mr Nampouno looked at her in surprise.

'Yes,' he said, 'as a matter of fact, I did dream. But why do you ask?'

'I just wondered,' said Annabel. 'What did you dream about?'

'I dreamt,' said Mr Nampouno, 'of my parents' house in Indonesia. I heard the birds in the garden and smelled the flowers and the delicious smells from my mother's kitchen. It was almost as if . . .' Suddenly he stopped and sniffed deeply. With his eyes open wide in surprise he looked at Annabel and Michael. 'But . . . but . . .' he said, 'I can still smell it!'

'That's right,' shouted Annabel and without further

ado she threw the door wide open, because she had heard footsteps on the stairs. Diana entered, carrying a large tray, and the other children followed her proudly.

'Here you are!' exclaimed Diana. 'The sun in a pan. Hurray! It was all Annabel's idea. Real *nasi goreng*!'

'And you have to eat it all up, because it's really good,' said Annabel. 'Mrs Dove says so, and she knows a lot about food. And Mr Fish . . . Mr Fish, who only really likes fish and chips, also tasted it. And do you know what he said? "The sun in a pan? Quite nice really, for a change!" '

Boiled Rice✱

200 g (8 oz) American or pre-fluffed rice
salt

1 Put the rice in a saucepan and cover it with cold water 2·5 cm (1 inch) above the level of the rice. Add a teaspoonful of salt.

2 Bring to the boil on a high heat and boil for 5 to 10 minutes until most of the water has boiled away. There should be bubbling holes on the surface of the rice.

3 Now cover the pan tightly with a lid and transfer it to another burner set on the lowest possible heat. Leave for about 20 minutes. This should give you perfectly cooked dry rice. (Leave to one side to cool if you're making *nasi goreng*.)

Nasi Goreng✱✱✱

1 onion
1 clove garlic
2 tablespoons vegetable oil
100 g (4 oz) finely sliced white cabbage
1 small red or green pepper, sliced, with the seeds removed or **some leftover cooked green beans or runner beans**
200 g (8 oz) cooked meat, chopped (You can use leftovers of beef, lamb, pork, chicken or ham – or you can use a combination of meats, but make sure that the total weighs at least 200 g.)
200 g (8 oz) cooked rice
1 tablespoon brown sugar dissolved in 1 tablespoon soy sauce
2–3 drops tabasco sauce (This is very **hot; you can**

leave it out if you want to.)
salt
2 eggs, salt, 1 tablespoon vegetable oil for the omelette
1 tomato and a few slices of pickled cucumber

1 Slice the onion finely and crush the clove of garlic.

2 Heat the oil in a large, deep frying pan or a heavy casserole and gently fry the onion and garlic until they are soft.

3 Add the cabbage and pepper or beans and cook gently for 5 minutes.

4 Add the meat to the vegetables.

5 Fluff up the rice and get rid of lumps by stirring it with a fork. Then add it to the frying pan and mix thoroughly.

6 Add the soy sauce and tabasco and season to taste with salt.

7 Stir the mixture all the time to make sure it's heated through and doesn't stick to the pan.

8 Keep the *nasi goreng* warm on a very low heat while you prepare the omelette (see page 42).

9 Cut the omelette into thin strips.

10 Transfer the *nasi goreng* to a serving dish and decorate it with strips of omelette and slices of tomato and pickled cucumber.

* *You can serve this dish with mango chutney and plain yogurt.*

Omelette ✱✱

2 eggs
salt
tablespoon vegetable oil

1 Beat the eggs and add a pinch of salt.

2 Heat the oil in a non-stick frying pan over a medium heat, pour in the eggs and cook until firm. Using a spatula, detach the omelette from the sides of the pan and slide it on to a plate.

Spring-cleaning

'Well, well, well . . .' said Mrs Dove, 'how pretty it all looks!' She stood on the threshold of the kitchen and clapped her hands in admiration.

'What do you mean?' asked Annabel's mother, who was standing on top of a ladder painting, with a scarf on her head. 'The kitchen or the garden?'

Mrs Dove peered at the garden through the open windows. 'Yes,' she said, 'the garden is lovely. I spend all day upstairs looking at the lilac tree. But I really meant the kitchen. It's going to look lovely. You'll be finished soon, won't you? We're going to have fun.'

'Yes,' said Annabel's mother with a sigh, and she sat down on top of the step-ladder looking round contentedly at the kitchen, which looked much brighter now that she and Diana had painted all the cupboards and shelves.

'We're going to have fun?' wondered Annabel, while she was helping Diana put the jars and pots back on the shelves.

' "Spring-cleaning done," ' said Mrs Dove, ' "we're going to have fun." That's what my mother used to say when the spring-cleaning was over; it was always a time of celebration. Because it was spring, and there was the horse-fair and the fun-fair in the village. Everything happened at once. My father would put a silver crown on the table to buy goodies as a treat after spring-cleaning. That was the tradition.'

'Treat? Who's going to get a treat?' That had to be Michael, of course. He and Mr Nampouno had been watering the garden – his ears always pricked up at any mention of goodies or treats.

'Pancakes?' he asked greedily.

'Pet,' said his mother, 'I shall be satisfied if I have time to warm up some leftovers for you this evening . . .'

'But you promised we would have pancakes at Whitsun!' cried Michael, 'and it's Whitsun now, isn't it?'

'But Michael, it's spring-cleaning too,' said Mrs Dove, who had been infected by all the busyness around her and who was handing Annabel the jars for the shelves.

' "Spring-cleaning done, we're going to have fun!" ' said Annabel to Michael. 'Don't scowl like that. When

we've finished we're going to have a surprise!' She winked at Diana, who winked back.

'What surprise?' asked Mrs Dove, Michael and Annabel's mother, all equally curious.

'Nothing,' said Annabel, 'but Diana and I and the others are going to give you all a treat, just like Mrs Dove's mother and father used to do.'

'Oh, no . . .' cried Annabel's mother. 'Not today, please! You're surely not going to start cooking in this clean kitchen? And what about the paint, Diana? The top shelves aren't even dry yet!'

Diana laughed. 'Who's talking about cooking?' she said mysteriously. 'It would be a pity to spoil our nice clean kitchen; in any case, I think it's much too warm to cook!'

'Sandwiches?' asked Michael, pouting.

'Wait and see,' said Diana, and stuck her head out of the kitchen window to call to Mr Nampouno, who was carrying the kitchen table back inside. 'No, no, leave it outside please. Today everything's happening outside! And everybody can help!'

'What's that?' rumbled Mr Fish, who was sitting under the lilac tree with his stamp albums. 'Me too?'

'You too!' Diana called back.

'And me?' asked Mrs Dove.

'And me?' asked Mr Nampouno.

'And me, and me, and me?' cried Bianca, Bas and Marion, who now appeared through the back gate with two laden shopping bags.

'I said everybody, didn't I?' chuckled Diana.

And, as usual, everything happened exactly as Diana had said. The plan had been agreed upon long before, and Bianca and Bas and Marion had already bought the shopping from a list written out the night before by Annabel and Diana.

'Never,' sang out Mrs Rosetta, who had just returned from a rehearsal at the opera, 'have I seen anything so lovely! Not even a cold buffet after a first night in Milan

looks like this!' With open arms she pointed at the splendid table spread with salads and snacks. 'Who made it all?'

'I chopped the parsley,' said Michael.

'And I cut the radishes into little roses,' Mr Fish said proudly.

'I bet you used your magnifying glass!' trilled Mrs Rosetta. 'They are beautiful, so dainty. Everything is beautiful! What a feast!'

' "Spring-cleaning done, we're going to have fun," ' said Michael, whose fingers were itching to poke the whipped cream decorating the fruit salad.

Corned Beef Salad ✱

1 small tin corned beef
10–12 small boiled potatoes
1 small beetroot cut into cubes
few sprigs of parsley
1 small onion
4 tablespoons mayonnaise
pinch of salt
2 hard-boiled eggs
lettuce leaves

1 Dice the corned beef and potatoes and put them in a bowl.

2 Add the cubed beetroot.

3 Wash the parsley and chop finely.

4 Peel the onion and chop finely. Add to the corned beef mixture with the mayonnaise, the salt and half the parsley, and mix well.

5 Put the bowl in the fridge for about 30 minutes.

6 Boil the eggs for about 9 minutes and then cool them quickly under the cold tap. Remove the shells and slice the eggs.

7 Wash and dry the lettuce leaves and put a few on each plate.

8 Just before you are ready to eat, spoon some of the corned beef mixture on to the lettuce and decorate with slices of hard-boiled egg, a small dollop of mayonnaise and the rest of the chopped parsley.

Celebration Fruit Salad ✱

1 whole fresh pineapple
6 fresh strawberries, cherries or plums
1 large apple
1 pear
1 banana
½ lemon
120 ml (5 fl oz) double cream with a little sugar added, whipped until stiff

1 Cut the pineapple in half.

2 Cut round the edges of the rind to loosen the fruit, taking care not to make any holes in the rind. Remove all the fruit from the two halves with a metal spoon.

3 Cut out and throw away the hard centre. Then cut the soft fruit into cubes and put it in a bowl.

4 Wash the strawberries, cherries or plums and remove the stones if necessary. If the fruit is large, cut it into small pieces and add them to the bowl with the pineapple cubes.

5 Peel, core and slice the apple and pear. Slice the banana.

6 Add the juice of the lemon to the fruit and mix gently with a spoon.

7 Fill the two hollowed-out pineapple halves with the fruit salad. If you want to make it even more mouth-watering, decorate the rims of the pineapple halves with small puffs of whipped cream.

A French Evening

Dring-g-g, dring-g-g . . . went the telephone.

Annabel's mother sighed. 'I wish the telephone couldn't be heard in the garden. I was so nice and comfortable here.'

'I'll go,' said Diana. 'It's probably for me.'

'No, I'm up now. I'll go,' said Annabel's mother, and she disappeared into the house.

'Was that the telephone?' Mrs Dove asked, who was sitting by the rose bushes under her parasol.

'Yes,' nodded Diana, 'but it's evidently not for one of us, otherwise she would have called by now.'

'It must be Mr Pradon,' said Mrs Dove, nodding her grey head.

Annabel looked up from the book she was reading to Michael. 'How do you know that, Mrs Dove?'

'Well,' said Mrs Dove, 'if it's someone having a long conversation with your mother, then it's bound to be Mr Pradon. Surely you know that.'

'But I thought Mr Pradon had gone on holiday,' said Diana. 'He always spends this time of the year in France.'

'We'll see,' said Mrs Dove, rocking gently in her cane rocking-chair. And, as always, she was right.

When Annabel's mother returned fifteen minutes later, she said immediately, 'That poor Mr Pradon! His sister has suddenly been taken ill, so he won't be in France for the fourteenth of July.'

'The what?' said Annabel.

'The fourteenth of July – Bastille Day. That's a great public holiday in France. There is music everywhere and people dance in the streets and everybody goes out to eat with their family. And because Mr Pradon is French, he always spends the fourteenth of July in Paris every year.'

'Oh,' said Annabel, 'that's why he talks so funny! I thought it was because he's so old.'

Mrs Dove laughed. 'I'm old too, but that doesn't mean I talk like Mr Pradon.'

'No,' said Annabel, 'that's true. But then why does Mr Pradon live over here if he is really a Frenchman, Mum?'

'Because he came over here to teach. Oh, a long time ago, certainly. He's been living over here for at least fifty years. When I was a little girl I had my first French lesson from Mr Pradon and even then he seemed like a very old gentleman to me. And every year before the summer holidays he would tell us about his trip and the fourteenth of July. I don't think he's ever missed a year. That's why I've invited him over to dinner tomorrow.'

'Tomorrow!' cried Annabel in dismay, rising red-faced from the grass. 'That's impossible, Mother. Tomorrow is the day we're going to put up a tent and make a camp-fire with Diana.'

'Yes, darling, but tomorrow is also the fourteenth of July. And we really must do something for Mr Pradon. We can make a camp-fire anytime during the summer holidays. And it really isn't suitable for such an old gentleman.'

Annabel nodded glumly and trailed slowly over to the garden gate to tell the children next door about the cancelled camp-fire, but Diana called her back.

'Say, Annabel, what would you think if we made a French party of it here tomorrow? With paper lanterns in the garden and a real French menu?'

Annabel's cheeks went red, no longer because of the heat, but with pleasure at Diana's idea. But Mrs Dove objected. 'French food? My darling child, don't you know that's the most difficult thing in the world? Surely we couldn't begin to do it properly? And certainly not the children!'

'Just you wait and see!' Diana called back.

Everybody forgot the heat and their laziness. Michael ran up to the attic to fetch the bunting. Mr Nampouno went off to look for real French music amongst the records, and Mr Fish stretched coloured washing lines between the trees to hang up the paper lanterns.

'Onion soup?' asked Annabel, who was lying on the grass, with the recipe notebook in front of her, compiling the shopping list. 'Is that nice?'

Mrs Dove wrinkled up her nose, but Annabel's mother called out that it was delicious and very, very French.

'And after that,' said Diana, 'what about lamb cutlets *à la grandmère*?'

'*A la* what?' Annabel jerked up her head in dismay.

Diana laughed. 'That's French,' she said. 'French for plain old lamb cutlets the way grandmother used to make them. I'm sure everyone will love them. Even Mrs Dove and Mr Fish!'

'Hey!' called Bianca and Bas from the garden gate, 'have you started writing down the recipes for the barbecue?' Bianca pronounced the word carefully, as Diana had taught them – 'bar-bee-queue'.

Bas threw himself down on the ground next to Annabel, who was scribbling away, and said, 'Why didn't you wait for us?'

'You're just in time,' said Diana. 'You can make the *mousse au chocolat* for tomorrow's French dinner in honour of Mr Pradon.'

The children stared at Diana, and of course Annabel had to explain about Mr Pradon and the fourteenth of July.

'And you mustn't be frightened off by that difficult name,' said Diana, 'because it's a chocolate pudding, and it's the loveliest thing in the whole world!'

'Non, non, non, non,' cried Mr Pradon in his solemn French tones the next evening, as he was sitting under the lanterns with a glass of wine. 'Non, non, I seemply

can't believe zat zee children 'ave concocted zees délicieux dinner!'

'What's "concocted"?' asked Annabel, while she danced with Michael under the light of the lanterns.

'Prepared,' laughed Diana, who was dancing with Mr Nampouno.

'And *délicieux*?' asked Bianca, who had a smear of chocolate mousse on the tip of her nose.

'Délicieux means delicious,' said Mrs Dove, who was rocking herself in time to the French music coming from the record player.

'No, not true!' cried out Marion, who was twelve and was learning French at school, 'Délicieux means yummy!'

Onion Soup ✱✱

1 small French loaf
6 medium onions
50 g (2 oz) butter or margarine
25 g (1 level tablespoon) brown sugar
25 g (1 rounded tablespoon) flour
2 beef stock cubes
salt and pepper
100 g (4 oz) grated cheese

1 Preheat the oven to 200°C (400°F), gas mark 6.

2 Cut the bread into slices about 1 cm (½ in) thick.

3 Peel and slice the onions.

4 Put the butter in a large saucepan and melt it over a medium heat. When the butter begins to foam, add the onions and sugar, cover and cook gently until brown.

5 Add the flour, stir and cook for a few minutes.

6 Add 1 l (2 pints) cold water, the stock cubes and salt and pepper, and stir until the soup starts to boil. Simmer gently for 10 minutes.

7 While the soup is simmering, take a deep ovenproof dish and cover the bottom with a layer of French bread. Scatter half the cheese on top, then cover with another layer of bread and scatter the rest of the cheese on top of that.

8 Remove the soup pan from the stove and pour the soup into the ovenproof dish over the bread and cheese. Put the dish in the middle of the hot oven and heat for 15 minutes.

9 Serve the soup, making sure everyone gets some bread and cheese.

Lamb Cutlets as Grandmother Used to Make Them ✵✵✵

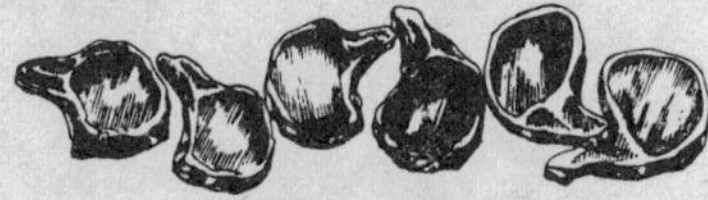

100 g (4 oz) bacon
100 g (4 oz) mushrooms
2 small onions
6 small tomatoes
few sprigs of parsley
500 g (1 lb) lamb cutlets
salt and pepper
50 g (2 oz) butter or margarine
1 small tin peas
1 small tin baby carrots

1 Cut the bacon into small pieces.

2 Wash the mushrooms very quickly and slice them if they are large.

3 Peel and slice the onions.

4 Wash and quarter the tomatoes.

5 Chop the parsley finely.

6 Rub the lamb cutlets with a little salt and pepper.

7 Melt the butter in a frying pan and fry the lamb cutlets on both sides until they are brown.

8 Put the cutlets on a plate. Reduce the heat and fry the onions and the bacon in the juices left in the pan.

9 When the onions have turned a light brown, add the mushrooms and fry for just a few minutes until they too are golden brown.

10 Add the tomatoes and simmer gently on a low heat for 15 minutes.

11 Put the drained carrots and peas with the cutlets in the frying pan.

Cover and heat gently for a few minutes.

12 Now serve up grandmother's special recipe in a nice large dish and sprinkle some parsley and more salt and pepper on top.

* *Fried potatoes are very nice with this recipe and can be served in the same dish.*

Chocolate Mousse✱✱✱

100 g (4 oz) plain chocolate
4 eggs
4 wafers

1 Break the chocolate into small pieces and put them with 2 tablespoons water in a heavy-bottomed saucepan over a *very* low heat. **Do not stir.**

2 Separate the eggs and put the whites into a large bowl.

3 Using an egg whisk, beat the whites until they are stiff enough to form peaks that will hold their shape.

4 When the chocolate has melted, stir it gently to make sure it is smooth and remove from the heat. Beat the egg yolks with a fork and add them to the chocolate.

5 Carefully add the chocolate mixture to the egg whites and mix them together with a folding motion, bringing the whites up over the

chocolate. Don't mix it too much, though, or you will lose all the air you have beaten into the egg whites.

6 Put the mousse into four small dishes and leave them in the fridge or a cold place for at least an hour before eating.

7 Serve with the wafers.

Indians and Palefaces

'Well, well,' said Mr Fish, 'are you getting yourselves ready for an expedition to the Himalayas?' He pointed at Bianca and Bas and Marion who were coming into the garden with heavy packs on their backs. Michael rushed over to greet them, but Annabel hung back to ask what the Himalayas were.

'Very high mountains, I think the highest mountains in the world, somewhere in India . . .' said Mr Fish vaguely.

'Oh,' said Annabel, 'is that where the Red Indians live?'

'No, no, no,' said Mr Fish, 'the Red Indians, Annabel . . .'

But Annabel had no more time for explanations. 'We are Indians, you see. Tonight we are going to live in a tent and eat around a camp-fire, and . . .'

Mr Fish looked a bit sour. 'Whatever next,' he said, shaking his head. 'I think that will mean you'll be crawling into your tent on empty stomachs tonight.'

'Ah!' said Annabel, 'just you wait and see! You're invited, you know, you're coming to eat with us tonight. You and Mrs Dove and everybody!'

Mr Fish looked even more glum. 'But surely you don't expect *me* to sleep in the wet grass?'

'Wet grass!' Annabel laughed. 'Can't you see the nice sleeping-bags we've all got?'

Mr Fish looked with astonishment at the sleeping-bags that were being rolled out on the grass by the children from next door.

'What will they think of next,' he said and, shaking his head, he disappeared through the garden gate on his way to the post office.

He was not the only one to have doubts about the Indian adventure. Annabel's mother had asked Diana at least four times whether it wouldn't be dangerous to have a fire in the garden, and Diana had answered at least four times that if the children did exactly what she told them to do, a barbecue would be just as safe as a gas or electric cooker.

'Well, I certainly wouldn't allow it if it weren't for you being there,' said Annabel's mother. 'At least you know all there is to know about fires and cooking.'

But Mrs Dove was not to be reassured so easily. She spent the whole afternoon nervously rocking herself in her rocker and craning her neck to see what was going on in the garden. And when dusk started to fall and the first puffs of smoke rose from the camp-fire, Mrs Dove anxiously squeezed the arm of Mr Nampouno, who was sitting beside her. 'Do you really think it's a good idea?' she asked anxiously. 'Meat on top of an open fire?'

Mr Nampouno sniffed very deeply and said, 'Well, to be honest, Mrs Dove, it smells just as nice as it does in the evening at home in Indonesia. That's the time of day that you can see small fires all along the road with men and boys selling meat on skewers. We call it *saté*.'

'Meat on skewers? Why not roast it normally, with lots of nice rich gravy?' interrupted Mr Fish, who had just come home from the post office and had joined them on the terrace.

'But just smell that wonderful aroma!' Mr Nampouno cried, excited by the smells coming from the back of the garden.

'Well, yes, perhaps I see what you mean . . .' Mrs Dove hesitated. 'In any case, I can't smell any food burning yet, Mr Fish.'

'No, no,' said Mr Fish uncertainly, and he threw an

unhappy glance at the room behind him, and the dining-table which today remained bare and unlaid. 'But why do *we* have to go along with all this nonsense?'

'There's no backing out now,' said Mrs Dove. 'I see the Indians are coming to fetch us.'

And so they were. Michael crossed the lawn with feathers stuck in a band around his curls. He bowed politely, and said, 'Redskin invite palefaces for lovely food.'

'Come on, Mrs Dove,' said Mr Nampouno, 'my mouth is watering!' He gave Mrs Dove his arm and walked with her to the Indian camp. Mr Fish followed with Annabel and Michael's mother.

'But how are we going to sit?' asked Mr Fish. 'You see, I prefer not to sit on the damp grass.'

'Oh, don't worry,' smiled Annabel's mother. 'See what comfortable seats have been provided for the palefaces.'

Annabel, also in a feather headdress, showed them one by one to the logs they had fetched from the shed, where they had been piled up waiting to be chopped up for firewood. Mrs Dove was even given a little cushion, and as soon as she was seated and saw all the tempting morsels on the grill above the glowing fire, she forgot all her worries and licked her lips just like Mr Nampouno as Marion put a couple of *saté* sticks and sauce on her plate. Mr Nampouno sat cross-legged on the ground amid the Indians, and his face shone.

'What a pity Mrs Rosetta is away on holiday,' said Diana, looking round the circle. 'I'm sure she would have known a lovely Red Indian camp-fire song.'

'In that case *I'll* sing you one!' rumbled Mr Fish.

'You?' exclaimed Mrs Dove, 'I thought you were in a bad mood, because you had to go without your nice rich gravy tonight!'

'But they gave me something even nicer!' chuckled Mr Fish, unwrapping a potato from its foil jacket and spreading butter on it.

'Me too!' said Annabel's mother. 'I have something even nicer in the kitchen. A surprise, a present from the palefaces to the Indians!' And when all the meat and potatoes were eaten the surprise was brought out: a large tub of icecream! The Indians broke into a wild dance with excitement.

'To be quite honest,' said Mr Fish, as the grown-ups returned to the house and the exhausted Indians crawled into their sleeping-bags, 'I must confess I wouldn't mind being an Indian myself tonight. How about you, Mrs Dove?'

Making a Fire

Never light a fire by yourself. Talk to grown-ups first about how and where you are going to build your fire. Always choose an open space at a good distance from leaves, wood or grass. Never light a fire under trees or near bushes and make sure the wind won't be able to fan your little fire into a great big blaze. Once your fire is alight, don't leave it *even for a moment*. Make sure there is always some water or damp sand at hand to put the fire out.

Take two large stones or bricks of similar size and place them in the shape of a V about 8 in (20 cm) apart. Make sure the wider end faces the direction the wind is coming from. Place a grill or a couple of iron bars across the top of the bricks and then put some dry sticks or twigs underneath as kindling. Light the kindling with a long taper and when it is burning, add dry logs, charcoal or special barbecue coal. If you have a ready-made barbecue, the same rules apply: **be very careful lighting your fire**.

If the weather is damp or windy, you may have to use a piece of cardboard or newspaper to fan the fire alight. Don't start cooking until the fire has died down to a mass of glowing embers.

Saté (Indonesian Kebabs)✱

200 g (8 oz) pork, lamb or beef
2–3 tablespoons olive oil
salt, pepper and garlic salt
thyme, marjoram and paprika
4 skewers

1 Cut the meat into small cubes.

2 Put the meat into a bowl and add the olive oil.

3 Add the seasoning, spices and herbs, and stir well.

4 Thread the meat on the skewers – about four cubes per skewer.

5 When the charcoal glows red, place the skewers on top of the barbecue grill. (Or you can cook the kebabs under the grill on a cooker.)

6 Turn the skewers every few minutes until the meat is brown all over. **Always use an oven glove when turning and removing the skewers from the heat.**

7 Serve the *saté* with the peanut sauce described below.

Peanut Sauce for Saté✱✱

4 tablespoons crunchy peanut butter
2 tablespoons olive oil
2 tablespoons desiccated coconut
juice of half a lemon
salt and pepper
1 tablespoon soy sauce
1 tablespoon brown sugar
1 drop tabasco sauce
(REMEMBER, **it's very hot; you can leave it out if you want to.)**
8 tablespoons milk or cream

1 Put the peanut butter with the olive oil in a heavy-bottomed saucepan and heat gently until the mixture is soft.

2 Add the coconut, lemon juice, salt, pepper, soy sauce, sugar and tabasco (if you are using it), and mix well.

3 Stirring constantly, add the cream or milk a little at a time. If the sauce seems too thick, you can add a little water to make it thinner.

4 Serve the sauce hot. People can dip their meat in it or you can pour it over the *saté* skewers before you serve them.

Kebabs✱

1 onion
2 tomatoes
1 green or red pepper
200 g (8 oz) lamb, cut into cubes
6 tablespoons oil
salt, pepper and garlic salt
thyme, marjoram and paprika
4 skewers

1 Cut the onion, tomatoes and pepper into pieces that are similar in size to the cubes of meat.

2 Mix the oil with the salt, pepper, herbs and spices in a big bowl and add the meat and vegetables. Stir well.

3 Take a skewer and thread it with a piece of meat, a piece of onion, another piece of meat, a piece of tomato, another piece of meat and a piece of pepper. Do this until each skewer is filled.

4 You can cook these kebabs on a barbecue in the same way you cooked the Indonesian kebabs or you can cook them under the grill on a cooker.

Sausages in Vests✱

6 frankfurter sausages
peanut butter
6 bacon slices

1 Slit the sausages from top to bottom but *don't cut them right through*.

2 Spread peanut butter inside and then close them up again and wrap a slice of bacon round each sausage.

3 Secure the bacon with a small skewer or a wooden cocktail stick and place the sausages on a hot barbecue or under the grill on a cooker. When the bacon is crisp on all sides, remove the sausages from the heat. Remember to use an oven glove so that you don't burn yourself.

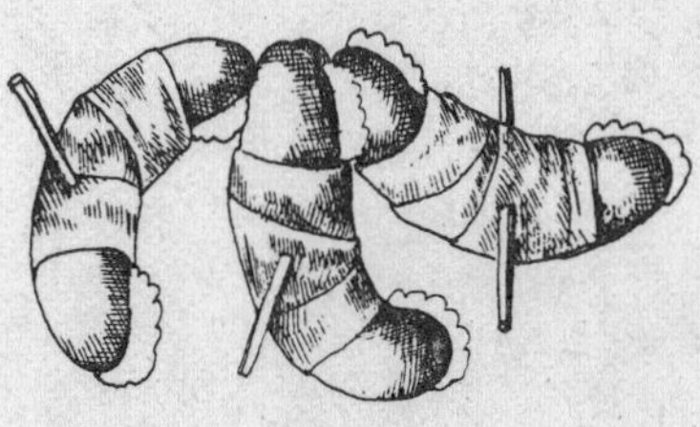

Parcels on the Fire✱✱

Food wrapped in aluminium foil and cooked in the glowing embers of a fire is always lovely, but remember that it takes *longer* to cook parcels this way than it does to cook them in the oven.

Recipes:

Chicken in a parcel (page 86)
Mackerel in a parcel (page 23)
Potatoes in a parcel (page 17)

There are other recipes in this book which don't have instructions for cooking in a parcel but which have a special flavour if you wrap them in foil and cook them in the embers. You can cook baked apples (page 73) in this way – and you'll soon discover lots of other possibilities.

The best accompaniments to a barbecue are baked beans, rice, sweet corn and green salad.

If you want to finish off with a real barbecue sweet, buy a bag of marshmallows and cook them one by one over the fire with a toasting fork until they are soft and sticky and slightly charred on the outside.

A Busy Day for Annabel

'Listen! Oh, listen!' said Annabel, with her finger pointing at the ceiling. 'I've never heard her sing so beautifully before!'

All the people in the room looked up and listened. Mr Fish lowered his newspaper, Mrs Dove rested the woollen hat she was knitting for Annabel in her lap, and Mr Nampouno, who was teaching Michael to play draughts, paused holding one of the pieces in his hand.

'You're right, you know,' said Diana, who was roasting chestnuts for everybody in the glowing embers of the open fire. 'Mrs Rosetta has never sung more beautifully.'

'It's in Italian,' said Annabel's mother. 'She only sings in Italian these days. I sometimes think . . .'

But what she sometimes thought was never revealed, because at that moment the phone started to ring in the hall.

'Bother!' said Annabel crossly, 'just when we were so cosy and enjoying the singing!'

Mrs Dove said, 'There's nothing as cosy as sitting round an open fire on a rainy October evening roasting chestnuts. When I was a little girl, I remember we would get a day's holiday from school to go and pick apples, and then in the evening we'd sit round the fire just as we're sitting now, and the whole house would fill up with the sweet smell of the apples, which my father would lay out on racks in the attic.'

'You must have eaten an awful lot of apple sauce,' said Annabel, who had half-heard while she was listening to her mother climbing the stairs and then Mrs Rosetta breaking off in the middle of a song.

'Oh, we had them in all sorts of different ways,' said Mrs Dove. 'We each took an apple to school every day, of course. And on Saturdays we'd have meat balls with apples that we had peeled, cut into slices and hung above the kitchen fire to dry. And then on Sundays . . . oh, on Sundays we'd have baked apples – delicious! I'm not sure that people these days know how to make such lovely baked apples, the way we used to make them. I say, Diana, would you like to include my recipe in your book?'

'Oh yes,' said Annabel, 'that's a lovely idea, we really must include one of Mrs Dove's old recipes, Diana!'

'Great! We'll have baked apples tomorrow,' said Diana. 'They sound scrumptious!'

'Can you remember any other old recipes from when you were a little girl?' Annabel asked. Mrs Dove reflected. 'Well, nothing springs to mind immediately, but I'll think it over.'

'What about an old remedy for sore throats?' asked Annabel's mother, who had returned. 'There was a gentleman on the phone for Mrs Rosetta just now – he was so hoarse I could hardly hear him!'

Just then Mrs Rosetta appeared in the doorway looking pale. In despair, she stretched out her arms to the people in the room, so that the ends of her silk shawl streamed down from her arms like a couple of bright wings. 'I am desperate,' she said. 'Mr Bastini, my partner in my big scene in the opera we are performing the day after tomorrow, has lost his voice!'

'Poor Mr Bastini! Poor Mrs Rosetta!' they all exclaimed, because they all knew how terribly important that opera was to both of them.

'It must be the damp weather,' said Annabel's mother, and Mr Fish added seriously, 'Especially for somebody who comes from Italy.' All Mrs Dove said was, 'Bull's eyes.'

They all stared at her in surprise, but Mrs Dove nodded firmly and said, 'Definitely. Bull's eyes, like my mother used to make them. It's the only cure I know for a lost voice.'

'Bull's eyes?' asked Mrs Rosetta, who had collapsed unhappily into the cushions of the couch beside Annabel, 'do you really think they might help, Mrs Dove? It's just that I feel so sorry for Mr Bastini, you understand . . .'

Mrs Dove laughed mischievously. 'Yes, I do understand, because you like him very much, don't you?'

Mrs Rosetta's cheeks turned bright red. 'How on earth did you know that?' she asked shyly.

'Well, Mrs Dove knows everything, doesn't she?' said Diana.

'Oh no,' said Mr Fish, 'not just Mrs Dove. I knew it too, because you've never sung more beautifully than you have in the past few weeks, Mrs Rosetta.'

'And in Italian, too!' added Mr Nampouno.

Mrs Rosetta's cheeks turned an even brighter red,

and Annabel and Michael crept towards her because it was the first time they had ever seen Mrs Rosetta looking shy.

'Then I might as well tell you now,' she smiled, 'Mr Bastini and I . . . I mean Marco and I . . .' Her laughter tinkled like a little tune.

Michael pulled at her shawl. 'Who's Marco?' he asked.

'Shush,' said Annabel, 'that's Mr Bastini, silly. Mrs Rosetta was just going to tell us that she and Mr . . .' She looked around her in surprise, because evidently all the grown-ups already knew what Mrs Rosetta was going to tell them. They had all jumped up and were kissing Mrs Rosetta's bright red cheeks or shaking her hand.

'We wanted to announce it after the evening of the opera,' Mrs Rosetta explained, 'but now . . .' Suddenly she looked miserable again. 'But now I don't know whether it will take place with that throat of his . . .'

'He'll get better,' said Mrs Dove. 'Bull's eyes! It's the only cure!'

'But surely the other thing, what you've just told us, that will happen anyway, with or without a voice?' said Diana.

'Of course!' cried Mrs Rosetta. 'Of course that will go on! And you are the first ones to know!'

'Except for us! We don't know anything! We don't know what you're talking about!' cried Annabel and Michael.

'Oh Annabel! Then it's about time you did know!' called Diana. 'Because tomorrow we shall cook real Italian spaghetti for Mr Bastini and his fiancée.'

'Has Mr Bastini got a fiancée?' Michael asked curiously. But Annabel, looking at Mrs Rosetta's happy face, suddenly put two and two together.

'Hurrah! hurrah!' she cried. 'What a busy day! Baked apples and spaghetti!'

'If that doesn't cure him, nothing will,' said Diana.

Spaghetti with Meat Sauce✱✱✱

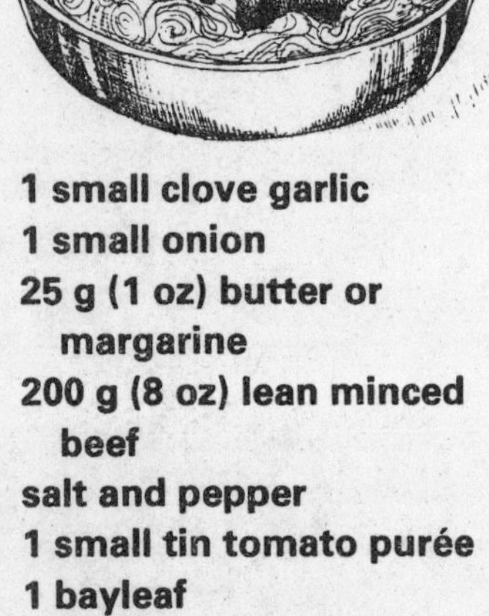

1 small clove garlic
1 small onion
25 g (1 oz) butter or margarine
200 g (8 oz) lean minced beef
salt and pepper
1 small tin tomato purée
1 bayleaf
1 tablespoon finely chopped parsley
200 g (8 oz) spaghetti
4 tablespoons grated Parmesan cheese (Cheddar will do)

1 Remove the papery skin from the garlic and the onion and chop them as finely as you can.

2 Melt half the butter in a saucepan. Add the garlic and onion and cook gently for a few minutes.

3 Add the minced meat, breaking it up into little pieces with a wooden spoon. Cook until brown, then add some salt and pepper.

4 Add the tomato purée, bayleaf, parsley and 125 ml (¼ pint) water. Simmer for a few minutes over a low heat.

5 Leave the sauce to cook gently for 10 minutes but stir it from time to time.

6 Boil a large saucepan of salted water and add the spaghetti. Leave to cook on a medium heat for 10 minutes or according to the directions on the packet. Stir it occasionally to stop it from sticking to the bottom.

7 Put the rest of the butter in a large serving dish and place in the oven to warm.

8 Drain the spaghetti in a colander over the sink. Put it in the warm dish.

9 Remove the bayleaf from the sauce and pour the sauce over the spaghetti. Sprinkle the grated cheese over the top and serve.

Baked Apples ✿

4 cooking apples
50 g (2 oz) brown sugar
½ teaspoon cinnamon
100 g (4 oz) raisins or sultanas
4 small marshmallows or 50 g (2 oz) red jam

1 Preheat the oven to 180°C (350°F), gas mark 4.

2 Slit the skins of the apples round the middle to prevent them from bursting. Remove the cores with an apple-corer.

3 Place the apples in a fireproof dish.

4 Mix the sugar, cinnamon and raisins together and stuff the middles of the apples with the mixture.

5 Put 4 tablespoons hot water in the bottom of the fireproof dish.

6 Bake the apples for at least 30 minutes or until they are soft. While they are cooking, baste them two or three times with the juices in the dish.

7 Remove the dish from the oven, put a marshmallow or a small blob of jam on top of each apple and serve.

A Sweet Month

'One, two, three, four . . . Into the jail! Mrs Dove goes to jail!' crowed Mr Fish. With his spectacles perched as always on the tip of his nose, he took Mrs Dove's little plastic counter, and slid it across the board.

'Poor Mrs Dove!' said Mrs Rosetta, 'and you were doing so well, too!'

'Never mind,' said Mrs Dove cheerfully. 'While I'm sitting in the jail I'll have time to eat another of those delicious apple fritters.'

Annabel quickly passed the plate piled high with apple fritters dusted in icing sugar.

'My goodness!' exclaimed Mrs Dove. 'I'm staggered every time I see that plate! To think that you children made those yourselves! Really . . .' She stopped to take an apple fritter and nibble it, nodding her head appreciatively. 'Just as good as my mother's.'

'And to think that last December none of them could even boil an egg,' said Annabel's mother.

'Nor even a potato,' said Mr Fish, who was moving his counter forward again.

'Do you remember when we started?' Diana asked Annabel.

She nodded. 'In February. The twelfth of February, when you were on TV. We wrote the date above our first recipe. Oh . . .' Annabel suddenly stood still, with her mouth wide open. 'But then . . . then it's been nearly a whole year! And you said that we had to cook for a whole year to make a book!'

'It's your go, Diana,' said Mr Nampouno, whose counter was a long way behind everyone else's in the game, because he had had to return to 'Go' twice.

'Hey, Annabel!' called her mother. 'Where are you going?'

'I'll be right back. You can throw the dice for me if you like,' called Annabel over her shoulder. 'I'm just going to get our recipe book.'

'But darling, surely you're not going to start writing recipes on New Year's Eve,' her mother objected when Annabel returned with the notebook.

'No, Mum. I just wanted to write down Mrs Dove's tip about draining the apple fritters. That made them nicer than when you make them.'

'Oh, thanks a lot,' said her mother, crestfallen. 'You're right, though. You see, Diana? You see what's happening? Now my daughter is teaching *me* how to cook!'

'I must be honest,' said Mr Fish, 'I confess I never believed it would work – these kids messing about in the kitchen, but after those apple fritters tonight, I take my hat off to you, children.' He made a polite little bow to Annabel and Michael, and also to Marion, who was celebrating New Year's Eve at their house.

'And those Christmas crown biscuits,' Mrs Dove said dreamily, 'Those were worthy of a master confectioner!'

'And what about that lovely fudge at Christmas!'

exclaimed Mrs Rosetta. 'Marco still won't believe that it was you who made that chocolate fudge, Marion!'

Marion's face shone, but Annabel, who was leafing through the recipe notebook, said seriously, 'Yes, but now it's time to make something savoury again, I think. We've made nothing but sweets for a whole month!'

'Well, yes, December is a sweet month, isn't it?' said Mrs Dove, who was munching on yet another apple fritter. 'Well, it suits me!'

'And me,' said Mr Fish merrily, and threw the dice on the table. 'Six!' he shouted. 'Six! I've won!'

'Twenty . . . thirty . . .' Annabel was counting out loud through all the din.

'What is that you're counting, Annabel?' asked Diana.

'The recipes of course,' said Annabel. 'I'm seeing whether we have enough yet for a book.'

'Hey!' her mother exclaimed suddenly. 'Why don't you count the strokes of the clock instead! Look, everybody, it's nearly midnight!'

And the recipe book was forgotten, because everybody in the house on the corner of Spoon Street stood up and waited eagerly for the first stroke of twelve. By the time the last stroke came, it could no longer be heard, because it was drowned by such a loud chorus of Happy New Years that in the kitchen Puss, the tomcat, woke up with a start.

Dutch Fudge ✵✵✵

150 g (6 oz) caster sugar
250 g (10 oz) granulated sugar
25 g (1 oz) cocoa
25 g (1 oz) butter

1 Grease a shallow baking tin.

2 Put all the sugar in a small saucepan and add the cocoa and 125 ml (¼ pint) water. Stir this mixture with a wooden spoon over a low heat until the sugar is dissolved. (When you scrape the bottom of the pan with your spoon the sugar should no longer feel gritty.)

3 Leave to cook gently and test from time to time by dropping a little syrup off the spoon back into the pan. When it no longer falls in a drop but dribbles in a tacky, fine thread, it is ready, so remove it from the heat.

Be very careful because you can burn yourself badly with boiling sugar.

4 Add the butter and stir the mixture well until it becomes thick and cloudy and you can see small sugar crystals forming. When this happens, pour the mixture as quickly as possible into the greased tin.

5 Leave the fudge to set and cut into squares when it is cold.

Christmas Crowns ★★★

1 egg
100 g (4 oz) butter or margarine
75 g (3 oz) caster sugar
150 g (6 oz) flour
pinch of salt
1 tablespoon granulated sugar
100 g (4 oz) flaked almonds

1 Preheat the oven to 180°C (350°F), gas mark 4.

2 Grease a baking tray.

3 Beat the egg in a small bowl.

4 Beat the butter or margarine with the sugar until light and creamy, using a wooden spoon.

5 Add half the beaten egg to the mixture and beat thoroughly.

6 Stir in the flour and salt.

7 Knead the ingredients together until the mixture forms a ball.

8 Scatter some flour on a clean work surface. Dust a rolling pin with some flour and roll out the pastry until you have a slab no thicker than 2 mm (⅛ inch).

9 Dust the rim of a pastry cutter or a glass in some

flour and cut out circles in the pastry.

10 With an apple-corer, thimble or bottle top cut a hole in the middle of each circle.

11 Carefully remove the biscuits and place them on the baking tray about 2 cm (1 inch) apart. Make a new ball from the leftover pastry, roll it out and make more biscuits. Do this until all the pastry is used up.

12 Brush the tops of the biscuits with the remaining beaten egg and scatter them with the sugar and flaked almonds.

13 Place the baking tray on the middle shelf of the oven and bake the biscuits for about 15 minutes until they are golden brown.

Apple Fritters ✱✱✱

100 g (4 oz) flour
pinch of salt
1 egg
250 ml (½ pint) milk
3 firm eating apples
½ teaspoon cinnamon
deep fat fryer one third filled with oil
icing sugar

1 Line a colander with kitchen paper and stand it on a plate.

2 Sift the flour and salt into a mixing bowl.

3 Make a well in the centre and drop in the egg.

4 Add half the milk and beat with a wooden spoon until the batter is smooth.

5 Gradually beat in the rest of the milk and then leave to one side.

6 Peel and core the apples. Cut them into rings about ½ cm (¼ inch) thick.

7 Sprinkle the cinnamon over the apple rings.

8 Heat the oil in a deep fat fryer. The oil is hot enough when it starts to give off a *very faint* grey haze. If the oil starts to smoke, you should remove it from the heat immediately. It's a good idea to have an adult helping you because **hot oil can be very dangerous**.

9 With two forks, take a slice of apple and dip it in the batter. Allow the excess to drip off and then carefully lower the apple into the hot oil. Do the same with each of the apple rings but don't put too many in at the same time.

10 Fry the rings until they are golden brown on both sides.

11 Drain them in the colander.

12 Put the apple fritters on a plate and sprinkle them with icing sugar. Serve them warm.

A Double Celebration

It was silent in the kitchen. Marion was glaring at Diana, and Annabel, sitting at the kitchen table, was tapping her pencil impatiently.

'But you can't have a birthday without cream cakes!' complained Bianca.

'No,' said Annabel. 'Diana and I have already made Michael's birthday cake, but we have to keep that as the sweet for after dinner. That means we haven't got anything to offer all the uncles and aunts who are coming to visit him this afternoon. And I was so looking forward to seeing their faces when they see our home-made cream cakes.'

'Never mind,' said Bas. 'Why don't we just make more of the peanut butter toffees. We don't need to use the oven for those!'

'I'm sorry,' said Diana, 'it's partly my fault. We should have remembered that we can't cook cakes *and* chicken in the oven at the same time. And we simply must make the chicken, because that's Michael's favourite.'

'And the peanut butter toffees as well,' said Annabel. 'Those are his favourite sweets. And we promised.'

'I wish we could cook cream cakes without an oven,' said Bianca.

'You can't cook cakes without an oven, silly,' snapped Annabel, but then Diana hit the table with her hand and exclaimed, 'That's it! I've got it! Ovenless cakes!'

Annabel gaped at her, amazed. 'Ovenless cakes? How do we do that?'

'Start writing,' said Diana. 'Take it down, and I'll explain. You'll have to prepare them on your own, though. I'm expecting a visitor in a moment.'

'A visitor? While we do the cooking? How are we going to cope without you?' Marion asked.

'Very well,' answered Diana. 'After all, you've cooked chicken in a parcel three times before. Everything is ready, and I'll light the oven for you. You've made peanut butter toffees before as well; the only thing you haven't tried before is the cream cakes, and I'm sure you can make those without me. I'll come back in half an hour to see how you're getting on. Start writing, Annabel.'

'Diana is right. We can manage perfectly well without her,' said Bianca after they had been busy for a while. She had chopped up the vegetables for the chicken, Bas was wrapping bacon round the chicken pieces, and Annabel and Marion had just finished preparing the toffees and were starting on the ovenless cakes. And at that moment the door opened and Diana appeared with a stranger.

'Hello, everybody,' said the gentleman.

Annabel turned round, feeling annoyed; Diana seemed to be acting very strangely today. First of all she had forgotten that you couldn't cook cakes and chicken in one oven at the same time, then she had simply walked out on them, and now she returned with a strange man to bother them! Annabel noticed that the man was watching her curiously, and then she became aware that she had forgotten a smear of peanut butter on her cheek. She felt herself blushing, and the gentleman said, 'You must be Annabel.' She nodded shyly. All the children looked up from their work.

'And do you know who *I* am?' he asked.

'No,' said Diana, 'I haven't told them yet. This is Mr Bos, children.'

'Hello, Mr Bos,' they all mumbled, while it was obvious they were all thinking to themselves, 'That's enough now. Goodbye, Mr Bos.' All of them, that is, except Annabel, who started to think, Mr Bos, Mr Bos? Who was that? The name rang a bell. Before she could get any further, Diana said, 'Mr Bos publishes my cookery books, remember? He is a publisher and I told him that you were writing a book too.'

Annabel blushed again. The publisher! The book they had been talking about for so many months! And now all of a sudden here was the publisher himself, in the kitchen, surrounded by the chicken and the cakes and the toffees cooling on a kitchen shelf! She quickly scanned the kitchen with her eyes. Was it looking tidy enough? Mr Bos seemed to follow her look.

'Mmm,' he said, 'everything looks absolutely delicious! May I try one of those toffees?'

'No,' said Annabel, 'you can't, Mr Bos. You'll have to wait for two hours. They have to cool down first.'

'Oh,' said Mr Bos, 'that's a bit too long to wait. But what about the notebook in which you've written all your recipes? May I look at that?' All the children left their tasks to crowd around Annabel as she handed the notebook to Mr Bos.

'Well, well,' he said. 'Have you really cooked all these things?' They all nodded and Bianca said, 'Some of them several times, because we liked them so much. And I have cooked everything I've learnt here again at my home, and my mother says she can't do it any better!'

'My mother says the same,' said Annabel.

'And mine,' said Marion.

Mr Bos laughed. 'Very good,' he said, leafing through the notebook, and reading bits here and there. 'Very good indeed. And are there any other notes?'

'Notes?' asked Annabel. 'No, this is our only notebook. Mr Nampouno gave it to us, and Mrs Dove covered it for us.'

She didn't understand why Diana and Mr Bos started to laugh at that, but Diana explained, 'He means things you write in addition to the recipes; notes on what you should and shouldn't do, and what you have to be careful about when you're cooking.'

'And all the things that went wrong?' cried Bas. 'Like when you put the frying pan on the stove with the handle sticking out!'

'Shhh,' said Annabel crossly, 'Mr Bos isn't interested in that.'

Everybody laughed, but Diana said, 'The children who will read our book will certainly be interested in that.'

'All right then,' said Annabel, 'we'll make some notes!'

'What are you going to make?' asked Mrs Dove on the threshold of the kitchen. 'Cakes?'

'No, a book!' shouted all the children, because the cakes and the toffees and the chicken had been quite forgotten.

'Oh . . .' said Mrs Dove, 'you mean, "What's Cooking in Spoon Street"!'

'Well,' said Mr Bos. 'I see you already know the title.'

'Mrs Dove always knows everything,' said Annabel.

Chicken in a Parcel✵✵

150 g (6 oz) soft butter
chives or spring onions
few sprigs of parsley
salt and pepper
4 small carrots peeled and finely sliced
1 chicken, jointed (five or six pieces)
slice of bacon for each piece of chicken
aluminium foil

1 Preheat the oven to 180°C (350°F), gas mark 4.

2 Put the butter in a bowl.

3 Finely chop the chives or spring onions and the parsley. Mix into the butter using a wooden spoon. Add the salt, pepper and carrots.

4 Spread the butter mixture on to the pieces of chicken and wrap a slice of bacon round each piece.

5 Wrap each piece of chicken in a piece of foil. Make sure the parcels are securely closed.

6 Place the parcels in an ovenproof dish and cook on the middle shelf of the oven for about 45 minutes.

7 Carefully unwrap one of the parcels and prick the chicken with a fork to make sure it is cooked.

8 When the chicken is cooked, remove the dish from the oven and serve the chicken pieces in the foil.

* *This dish goes well with a green salad and rice or French bread warmed up in the oven.*

Ovenless Cakes✱✱

200 g (8 oz) soft butter
200 g (8 oz) icing sugar
few drops of vanilla essence
1 dessertspoon powdered instant coffee
200 g (8 oz) digestive biscuits
hundreds and thousands or a little finely grated chocolate

1 Put the butter in a bowl and beat it with a wooden spoon until it is soft and creamy.

2 Sieve the icing sugar into the bowl. Add the vanilla and mix well.

3 Divide the butter cream into two equal parts and put one half into a second bowl.

4 Dissolve the instant coffee in a cup with half a tablespoon of boiling water. When cool, stir it into the butter in the second bowl.

5 Spread a thick layer of the coffee-flavoured butter on a biscuit and press a second biscuit on top to make a sandwich. Make several more biscuit sandwiches until all the coffee filling is used up.

6 Decorate the top of the biscuit sandwiches with the vanilla-flavoured butter cream. Do this with a knife or an icing tube. (If you have an icing tube you can make little whirls with the cream or you can even make letters.)

7 Finally, scatter some hundreds and thousands or finely grated chocolate over the decorated cakes.

Peanut Butter Toffees ✱

150 g (6 oz) plain chocolate
150 g (6 oz) soft toffees
1 tablespoon milk
4 tablespoons peanut butter
125 g (5 oz) cornflakes

1 Melt the chocolate and the toffees with the milk in a heavy-bottomed saucepan over a *very* gentle heat.

2 Take the saucepan off the heat and add the peanut butter. Continue stirring.

3 Add the cornflakes and stir until well mixed.

4 Using two teaspoons, scoop little mounds of the mixture on to a plate. Leave the sweets in a cool place for about two hours or until they have cooled and are hard.

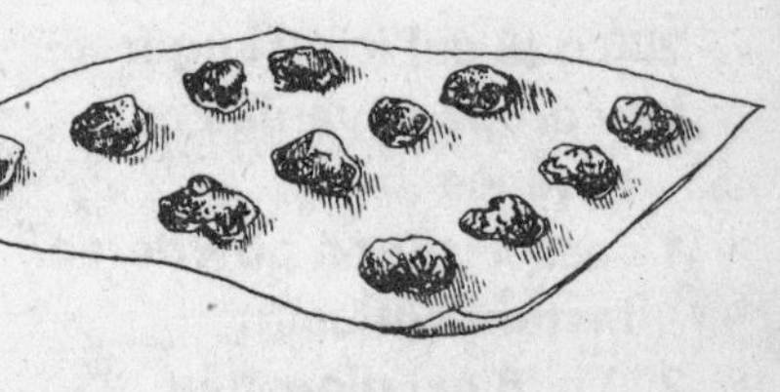

Apple Purée ✱

3 large cooking apples
pinch of cinnamon
drop of vanilla essence
50 g (2 oz) sugar

1 Peel the apples and cut them into quarters. Remove the stalks and cores.

2 Put the apples and 125

ml (¼ pint) water in a saucepan, cover with a lid and cook over a low heat.

3 When the pieces of apple are quite soft, remove the saucepan from the heat.

4 Place a sieve over a bowl and put the apples in the sieve. Stir them with the back of a spoon until they have all been pushed through the sieve.

5 Stir in the cinnamon, vanilla and sugar. If you want to make it even more scrumptious, add a tablespoon of cream.

Index

Some other Puffins

COOKING IS A GAME YOU CAN EAT

Fay Maschler

Cooking is the very best game of all: for once you have had the fun of weighing and mixing, chopping, rolling, kneading, shaping and decorating, and cooking, you can eat the results!

Fay Maschler has collected together some delicious recipes for all kinds of food; for cooking indoors and out; for when you are bored on a rainy afternoon, and for taking on expeditions. You can make kebabs and toast marshmallows round a campfire; discover real cowboy hash, '1000-year-old' eggs and Gratie Taties. Ice-cream is surprisingly easy to make, and have you ever eaten Rocky Road? You can treat someone to breakfast in bed, make your own edible Christmas decorations and impress your family and friends with a bowl of exotic sparkling fruit. If you follow the rules carefully, the results will be delicious.

THINGS TO DO

Hazel Evans

Bored on a rainy afternoon? Fed up with playing the same old games? Perhaps you're on holiday in the country or in a big city and don't know what to do? Then be a magician; keep an indoor zoo or start a bonsai tree. Make your own guitar, design a glove-puppet or make an orange-peel belt. Try phoning a friend on your own home-made telephone or start a treasure hunt, practise brass rubbing or grow a 'squirting cucumber'!

Everything in this book has been thoroughly tried and tested by the author and her family. You need not buy expensive materials and, though the ideas are simple and practical, they are great fun to carry out.

ALL THE YEAR ROUND

Toni Arthur

Television presenter and singer, Toni Arthur, has compiled an incredible variety of traditional customs and stories, songs and games to keep you occupied and interested during even the greyest times of the year. There are bits of folk lore from all over Britain which make you realize what a rich and peculiar past this country has. But whilst informing and entertaining you with traditional stories and pastimes, Toni is ever practical. She tells you how to make anything from a sock puppet to cinnamon toast, and she also reveals the secret of invisibility and a foolproof method of keeping witches away.

PLEASURE WITH PAPER

A. van Breda

No more hunting for outsized cardboard boxes or searching for two dozen bottle-tops at the crucial moment. All you need is paper, a pair of scissors, glue and a pot or two of paint. If you can lay your hands on these, you can create a whole paper world for yourself. Model animals, a miniature village, a family of dolls with their clothes and decorations for your home are just some of the ideas which you can get from this book.

A. van Breda's instructions are clearly explained and the detailed illustrations will help children of all ages to make these models on their own.

Heard about the Puffin Club?

. . . it's a way of finding out more about Puffin books and authors, of winning prizes (in competitions), sharing jokes, a secret code, and perhaps seeing your name in print! When you join you get a copy of our magazine, *Puffin Post*, sent to you four times a year, a badge and a membership book.
For details of subscription and an application form, send a stamped addressed envelope to:

The Puffin Club Dept A
Penguin Books Limited
Bath Road
Harmondsworth
Middlesex UB7 0DA

and if you live in Australia, please write to:

The Australian Puffin Club
Penguin Books Australia Limited
P.O. Box 257
Ringwood
Victoria 3134